IN APPRECIATION OF HIS WORK, FOR DR. TONY WOOD —S. M.

FOR MY FATHER, NORMAN SAUNDERS,
WHO GAVE ME THE COURAGE TO TRY MY BEST —Z. S.

ACKNOWLEDGMENTS
The author would like to thank Duncan M. Porter, Director, Darwin Correspondence
Project at Virginia Polytechnic Institute & State University, for sharing his enthusiasm
and expertise.

As always, a special thank-you to Skip Jeffery for his help and support throughout
the creative process.

Book design by Katie Jennings.
Typeset in Scriptoria and New Renaissance.
The illustrations in this book were rendered
in mixed media.
Manufactured in China.

10 9 8 7 6 5 4 3 2 1

Chronicle Books LLC
680 Second Street
San Francisco, California 94107

www.chroniclekids.com

Library of Congress Cataloging-in-Publication-Data
Markle, Sandra.
Animals Charles Darwin saw : an around-the-world
adventure / by Sandra Markle ; illustrated by
Zina Saunders.
p. cm.
ISBN 978-0-8118-5049-0
1. Darwin, Charles, 1809–1882—Juvenile literature.
2. Naturalists—England—Biography—Juvenile literature.
3. Animals—Juvenile literature. 4. Beagle Expedition
(1831–1836)—Juvenile literature. I. Saunders, Zina.
II. Title.
QH31.D2M37 2009
576.8'2092—dc22
[B]
2007053058

ANIMALS
Charles Darwin
SAW

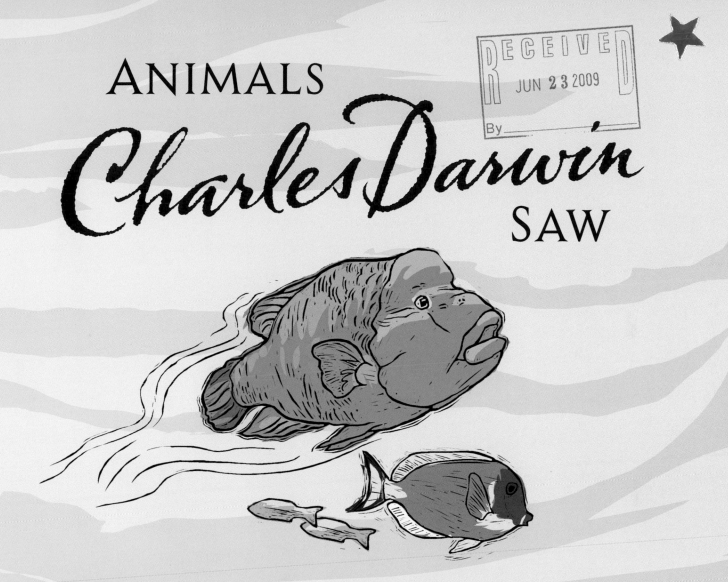

AN AROUND-THE-WORLD ADVENTURE

By Sandra Markle

Illustrated by Zina Saunders

chronicle books · san francisco

NOTE TO PARENTS AND TEACHERS

The books in the Explorers series take young readers back in time to share explorations that had a major impact on people's view of the world. Kids will investigate why and how the explorers made their journeys and learn about animals they discovered along the way. They'll find out how some animals affected the outcome of the journey, helping explorers find their way, causing key events to happen, or helping the explorers survive. Young readers will also learn that, because of the explorers' journeys, animals were introduced to places they'd never lived before, sometimes with dramatic results.

The Explorers series helps students develop the following key concepts:

From the National Council for the Social Studies:
Human beings seek to understand their historical roots and to locate themselves in time. Such understanding involves knowing what things were like in the past and how things change and develop. Students also learn to draw on their knowledge of history to make informed choices and decisions in the present.

From the National Academy of Sciences:
Making sense of the way organisms live in their environments will develop an understanding of the diversity of life and how all living organisms depend on the living and nonliving environment for survival.

CONTENTS

THE BIG IDEA

Imagine you're walking along a beach and find a lot of really big bones—enough to form a whole animal's skeleton. When you put the bones together, the body is shaped like a rat, but it's the size of an elephant! Think about how strange such a discovery would seem, especially if you'd never seen any rats this size before. Where could it have come from? Is it possible you've discovered a whole new kind of animal? If you lived before Charles Darwin proposed his theory of evolution (EH-vuh-loo-shun), you might think so.

Before Darwin, people did not believe that animals changed over time. But after Darwin stumbled on some strange bones, he started thinking. He thought about the many different kinds of wildlife he had observed and how the animals seemed well suited to the environments in which they lived. He began to wonder whether animals did change over time, developing the characteristics they needed to survive and prosper.

Of course, not everyone agreed with Darwin's theory that living things change over time. In fact, the debate continues today. So how did Darwin come up with the idea of evolution? You may be surprised to learn about the different animals that played a key role in the development of his theory.

SEA MONSTERS

Charles may have seen some strange-looking deep-sea fish, such as the gulper eel and giant squid. Typically, gulper eels are 5 feet (1.5 meters) long, and their jaw takes up nearly one-fourth of their total length. Giant squid can be nearly 40 feet (12 meters) long, including their tentacles, which are covered with hundreds of suckers ringed with tiny teeth.

GROWING UP EXPLORING

Charles Darwin was born in Shrewsbury, England, on February 12, 1809. He grew up in the country and spent his playtime exploring the woods and fields near his home. He also loved collecting anything interesting that he found, such as shells, rocks, plants, insects, and birds' eggs.

When he was 16, Charles's father sent him to Edinburgh University in Scotland to study medicine. Both his grandfather and his father were doctors, so Charles's father thought Charles should be a doctor, too. But Charles wasn't very interested in his classes. He spent more time going for walks and observing wildlife than studying. Sometimes he also sailed with local fishermen to see what strange creatures they pulled up in their nets.

When he was 18, Charles told his father that he didn't want to be a doctor. His father decided he should be a clergyman—a religious leader in the Christian church—instead, and sent him to Cambridge University in Cambridge, England. But once again, Charles was far more interested in exploring than studying. He also discovered he could make money by collecting beetles. It had become fashionable for people to collect and display beetles, and the rarer the beetle, the more money it fetched.

Once, with two unusual beetles in hand, Charles spotted a third. Determined to collect all three to sell, he held on to one beetle, popped the other into his mouth, and then reached for the third. Suddenly, the insect in his mouth released a burning liquid. Shocked, Charles spat it out and dropped the other two beetles. He had just learned an important lesson: always take time to observe an animal and understand its behavior before drawing any conclusions about it.

BUG BOMB

The beetle Charles put in his mouth was probably a bombardier beetle. To defend itself, this insect fires two chemicals from its rear end. These chemicals mix in the air to form a stinky, boiling-hot liquid.

The Chance of a Lifetime

In 1831, Charles graduated from Cambridge University. Before he could find a job as a clergyman, he received a letter that would change his life. He was offered a job as an assistant to the naturalist—a scientist who studies plants and animals—onboard the HMS *Beagle*, a British navy ship. John Henslow, his botany teacher at Cambridge, had been impressed with Charles and recommended him for this job. The main goal of the voyage was for the crew to survey the coast of South America, then continue around the world, taking measurements to help improve the charts and maps used by navy ships. But the naturalist on the voyage would also study wildlife and collect samples. Charles was thrilled to have a job that would let him observe nature and travel to parts of the world that he'd never seen before.

At first, Charles's father refused to let him go. The voyage was supposed to last for two years, and Charles's father thought it would be a waste of time. But Charles's uncle, Josiah Wedgwood, convinced him to let Charles go. On December 27, 1831, Charles sailed from Plymouth, England, onboard the HMS *Beagle*. His big adventure had begun!

STUFF IT

Part of Charles's job was to stuff the animals he collected on the trip. In the 1800s, explorers and hunters took the skins of animals they killed to upholstery shops to be sewed up and stuffed for display. While at Edinburgh, Charles had taken private lessons in this process, called taxidermy (TAK-suh-dur-mee). So he was already prepared for this part of his job.

LAND AT LAST

The *Beagle* sailed south and, on January 16, 1832, stopped at Santiago Island, one of the Cape Verde Islands off Africa. When part of the crew went ashore, Charles went along. He'd been very seasick and was happy to be on solid ground again. He was also thrilled to walk away from the beach and into a grove of coconut palms; it was the first time he'd been in a tropical place. He saw birds, insects, and lizards that were very different from any he'd ever seen before. But he was especially interested in the octopuses he saw in tidal pools. Sometimes the octopuses squeezed their bodies into crevices that seemed too small for them. And when they sat still on a rock, Charles had to pull hard to drag their bodies off. His biggest surprise was seeing an octopus change color. In a flash, this animal's color could change to blend in with its surroundings.

FEELING COLORFUL

An octopus can change color because its skin is packed with lots of special pigment-filled cells. These are like tiny bags full of colored pigments: yellow, red, blue, or black. When the muscles around a cell contract, the cell is pulled into a flat plate and the color is displayed. Octopuses change color to hide. But they also change color when they are upset or excited.

17

BEETLE FARMERS

Still interested in beetles, Charles probably collected dung beetles in Brazil. These beetles plant rubber trees in the rainforests. But they do not do it on purpose. First, monkeys eat the rubber tree's fruit. The seeds pass through their bodies unchanged and are deposited with their wastes. Dung beetles roll the waste into balls. Then the beetles bury the balls to eat later. For the seeds, this is like being planted with a bit of fertilizer.

WILD IN BRAZIL

On April 4, 1832, the *Beagle* reached Rio de Janeiro, Brazil. Charles temporarily left the ship to study the plants and animals that lived there. While the *Beagle* sailed north to survey the coastline, Charles explored a junglelike forest with colorful birds, insects, and monkeys. Unlike the woodlands he'd explored as a boy in England, this forest appeared to be home to a surprising number of different kinds of animals.

When he returned to the *Beagle*, the ship's naturalist had gone home. The position was now Charles's.

During the remainder of 1832, Charles traveled with the ship, exploring and collecting at each stop. Because the captain complained about all the samples piling up, Charles sent some of them home to make room for more.

On the beach in Punta Alta, Argentina, Charles discovered unusually large bones mixed in with the gravel and mud. He would later come back to dig up the bones and ship those home, too. They would turn out to be an important discovery.

HOME ON THE PAMPAS

In 1833, Charles explored Chile, Argentina, and Uruguay. While he was in Argentina, he traveled with cowboys, called gauchos (GOW-chohz), and investigated the vast grassland area called the pampas (PAM-puz). Far inland, he was amazed to discover shallow saltwater lakes that were home to flocks of long-legged pink birds—flamingos.

Close to the rugged Andes Mountains, Charles saw llamas. Related to camels, llamas are sure-footed on rugged ground and therefore perfectly suited to the environment in which they live. If he got too close, Charles probably learned another valuable lesson about this unfamiliar animal. When upset, a llama spits a foul-smelling mouthful of its stomach contents at whatever is annoying it.

On August 22, 1833, Charles traveled back to Punta Alta—back to the mysterious giant bones.

WHY ARE FLAMINGOS PINK?

Flamingo chicks have gray feathers. The adults are colorful because of what they eat. They use their big beaks to scoop up algae and tiny crustaceans such as shrimp. Both contain carotenoid (KEH-rah-teh-noid) pigments, like the pigments that color carrots. Eating lots of these pigment-rich foods makes their feathers red or orangish-pink.

Giants on the Beach

When Charles returned to Punta Alta, he was amazed to find not just bones, but giant skulls. In all, he found pieces of nine different animals, and for some, he had enough to put the animal's complete skeleton together. One looked something like an armadillo's skeleton, but it was as big as a rhinoceros! Another skeleton looked as if it might have belonged to something like a rat—but it was as big as an elephant! He guessed that these were skeletons of animals that were extinct (IK-stingkt), or no longer living today.

The fact that these skeletons looked similar to living animals made Charles wonder if the extinct animals might be related to ones alive today. That could mean two things: the animals currently living are not the only animals that ever existed, and it is possible that animals change—or evolve— over time. These were new ideas. Like many people at the time, Charles had been raised to believe that each animal is created in its present form and does not change over time. But as he packed up the bones to send back to England on another ship, he wondered why none of these giant animals were living today. What had happened to them?

SUPER SLOTH

Darwin also discovered the bones of a sloth as big as an ox. By comparison, sloths living today are only about 20 inches (50 centimeters) long. Today's sloths climb trees to eat leaves, but a giant sloth probably snagged tree limbs with its big claws and pulled them down to grab a mouthful.

SHAKE AND BAKE

Continuing on its mission, the *Beagle* traveled around the tip of South America and reached Valparaíso, Chile, on July 23, 1834. Once again, Charles set off to explore the land. Some distance from the sea, he discovered huge beds of seashells, and he wondered how these had gotten so far above sea level.

Later, Charles was resting in a wood when the ground under him shook. It was an earthquake. There was little damage in the wood, but when he rode into a city called Concepción (kon-sep-see-OHN), Charles found that many houses had been reduced to rubble. Along the shore, he discovered mussels that had once been underwater in tide pools clinging to rocks that were far above the reach of even the highest tide. They were rotting in the hot sun. Seeing this made Charles think about the beds of seashells he had seen. And he thought about the bones he'd found of animals that were no longer alive. He wondered if changes in the earth's surface could possibly affect the animals living on it.

LIFE ON THE EDGE

Mussels living in tidal pools at the edge of the sea need to stay moist to survive. At low tide, when the water recedes, mussels pull their two shells tightly together to keep some water inside. At high tide, when the water comes back, it carries the tiny plants and animals that mussels eat. The mussels open their shells and their gills filter this food out of the water.

BUG ATTACK

While camping in the pampas, Darwin was bitten by a blood-sucking black bug called a benchuca (BEN-chu-kah). He watched with interest as the skinny bug swelled up with his blood. He then kept the insect in a box for about six weeks. When it was skinny again, he let it bite his finger to watch it swell up once more. Today, this insect is known to pass on parasites that cause Chagas' (SHAH-gus) disease, which causes intestinal problems and heart disease. This bite may be the reason Darwin was often sick later in life.

Charles's curiosity grew during the several treks he made high into the Andes Mountains in Chile. During these expeditions, he discovered more seashells embedded in rocks high in the mountains and far from the sea. Again he wondered if the seashells were there because the earth had changed.

When Charles went down the other side of the mountains, he discovered something else that interested him. One side of the Andes faces the Pacific Ocean, and the other faces the Atlantic. Charles discovered that each side has a different climate and is home to very different plants and animals. Charles found mice on both sides of the Andes, but those on the Pacific side were different from those on the Atlantic. He wondered if specific mice were created for each side of the mountain, or if the mice had evolved to survive in different conditions.

A WORLD OF THEIR OWN

Continuing on its voyage of exploration, the *Beagle* reached the Galápagos Islands on September 15, 1835. This group of small volcanic islands is separated from South America by nearly 600 miles (965 kilometers) of ocean. The islands are also just far enough apart that most animals don't migrate—or travel—between them, so each island is its own world. But the islands do have some things in common. Lying just south of the equator, they all get a lot of sun, and each island has the same shrubby trees and weeds. The insects and dull-colored birds Charles collected there looked similar, too. So did the giant tortoises.

TELL A TORTOISE BY ITS SHELL

The people living on Charles Island (now Isla Santa María) in the Galápagos hunted the tortoises for their meat. They claimed they could tell which island a tortoise came from by looking at its shell. Later, that comment would be helpful to Charles.

ONE-OF-A-KIND LIZARD

Charles was fascinated by watching marine iguanas, the only iguanas in the world that live and feed in the sea. He found it interesting that this iguana's webbed toes and flattened tail were just what it needs to be a strong swimmer. Its land-living cousin has a round tail and toes with strong claws—just what it needs to climb around on the rocky ground.

Charles did not think the animals he collected in the Galápagos were very interesting, but they did make him wonder. He thought about the fact that while each island had similar kinds of birds, tortoises, and iguanas, the animals varied slightly from island to island. Just as with the plant and animal life he observed in the Andes Mountains, he wondered if different kinds of animals were created for each island, or if the animals are different because the islands they lived on all have their own unique environments.

HOME AT LAST

Finally, on October 20, 1835, the *Beagle* left the Galápagos Islands and headed home. The voyage that was supposed to take only two years had already lasted four. Because the *Beagle* took the long way home, sailing most of the way around the globe, the homeward trip took almost another year. This time, the stops it made included brief visits to Tahiti, New Zealand, and Australia. In each of these places, Charles studied the coral reefs. He was fascinated by the colorful fish he saw swimming in the shallow water over these reefs, and he wondered how the reefs had formed.

When the *Beagle* made a quick stop at Ascension Island in the South Atlantic, Charles found mail waiting. His sister wrote that his teacher John Henslow had published a book of the letters Charles had sent him describing his voyage. The book was popular, and everyone was talking about his scientific work and discoveries. Charles was shocked and happy about the news. When he returned to England on October 2, 1836, other scientists treated him with respect. He was asked to join the Royal Society of London, England's leading group of scientists.

REEF UNDER CONSTRUCTION

Darwin learned that tiny animals create coral reefs. Each coral animal produces a hard skeleton around itself. When it dies, its skeleton becomes the foundation on which new coral animals build. Slowly, the coral colony becomes big enough to form a reef.

Charles was happy to be home, but after a short visit with his family, it was time to go to work. He had boxes and bottles full of thousands of preserved birds, lizards, insects, spiders, and other animals. They needed to be sorted and studied. Luckily, with his new reputation as a scientist, Charles was able to get highly respected experts to help. It was bird expert John Gould who told Charles some surprising news. A group of birds from the Galápagos Islands that Charles thought were different kinds were actually all finches. And these finches were related to finches found in South America, 600 miles (965 kilometers) away from the Galápagos.

How could that be? Charles guessed that a storm had blown some South American finches to the Galápagos Islands. Slowly, over time, the finches developed different features to help them survive in their new island homes. This, and his other thoughts about the strange animals he'd seen on the voyage of the *Beagle*, led Charles to an idea he called transmutation (trans-myu-TAA-shun). Today we call it the theory of evolution. Evolution is the process by which something changes in stages from one form to another.

DARWIN'S MOCKINGBIRDS

Charles also discovered each of the Galápagos Islands had its own variety of mockingbird. While finches may migrate from island to island, mockingbirds tend to claim a territory and stay home. Studying them made Darwin think about how mockingbird varieties differ. He considered how those differences make the birds especially suited to their environments. He began to wonder whether a process of evolution might be responsible for these differences.

SURVIVAL OF THE FITTEST

Several years after his return to England, Charles married and became a father. He was often sick, but when he was well, he continued to study different kinds of plants and animals. He wanted to understand what causes living things to change to fit their environments. Charles thought about the tropical forests he had visited, which were full of lots of different kinds of animals and plants.

Charles also studied barnacles to understand all the differences that can exist within one group of related animals. He observed that animal families produce lots of slightly varying offspring. He realized that having different traits means that some barnacles are better suited than others to catching food and escaping hungry predators. Then, when they produce offspring, they pass on their special traits to the next generation. This Darwin described as natural selection or "survival of the fittest." This concept helped him better understand how animals can change over time.

ALL THE BARNACLES

A barnacle (BAR-ni-kul) is a kind of marine shelled animal related to clams and oysters. The young are free-swimming, but when they become adults, they permanently attach themselves to something solid, such as a rock on the seafloor or even a ship's hull. There are nearly a thousand different kinds of barnacles, and Darwin studied them all. It took him eight years.

WAR OF WORDS

Charles knew his theory of evolution would upset many people. He also realized his theory could be considered an important scientific discovery. He wanted to be sure he, and not somebody else, received credit for thinking of it. So while he didn't try to publish his theory, he wrote it down and sent it to one of his most trusted friends. Then what he feared might happen did. A young scientist named Alfred Russel Wallace sent a letter asking Charles's opinion of a theory that Wallace had. Charles was stunned. Wallace's theory was almost exactly the same as his own theory of evolution.

Charles asked his scientist friends what he should do. They decided to make both Darwin's and Wallace's theories public so both could get credit for the new idea. They did this at a meeting of important scientists.

Just as Charles had feared, the idea of evolution launched a big debate. Some supported the idea that animals and plants have changed over time. Others were strongly against it, believing each living thing was created exactly as it is today.

THE PEPPERED MOTH

Peppered moths living in Great Britain show evolution in action. In the early 1800s, most peppered moths had white wings with black spots. To hide from hungry birds, they rested on trees that had white-and-black-colored trunks. Then factory smoke covered the trees with black soot. Before long, most peppered moths were dark with light spots. Then antipollution efforts cleaned up the trees. By the 1990s, there were once again many peppered moths with white wings and black spots.

A World Changed Forever

In 1859, Charles published a book called *On the Origin of Species* to explain the reasons he believed in evolution. He never suggested that people had evolved, but because the skeletons of ancient people look similar to the skeletons of apes, some people jumped to the conclusion that the theory of evolution meant people had evolved from apes. That caused even more arguments. Charles was unhappy to have angered people, but he was pleased to receive credit for a theory that launched a whole new field of study—the study of how traits are passed from parents to offspring. This branch of science is called genetics (juh-NEH-tiks).

The debate over evolution continued after Charles's death in 1882. It continues today. Sometimes the idea of evolution still makes people angry. But whether people believe in evolution or not, Charles Darwin's theory has forever changed the way the world is viewed. And people are aware that, for better and for worse, there is a relationship between living things and their environment.

MAP OF THE *BEAGLE'S* VOYAGE

Follow the arrows to track Charles Darwin's voyage on the *Beagle*.

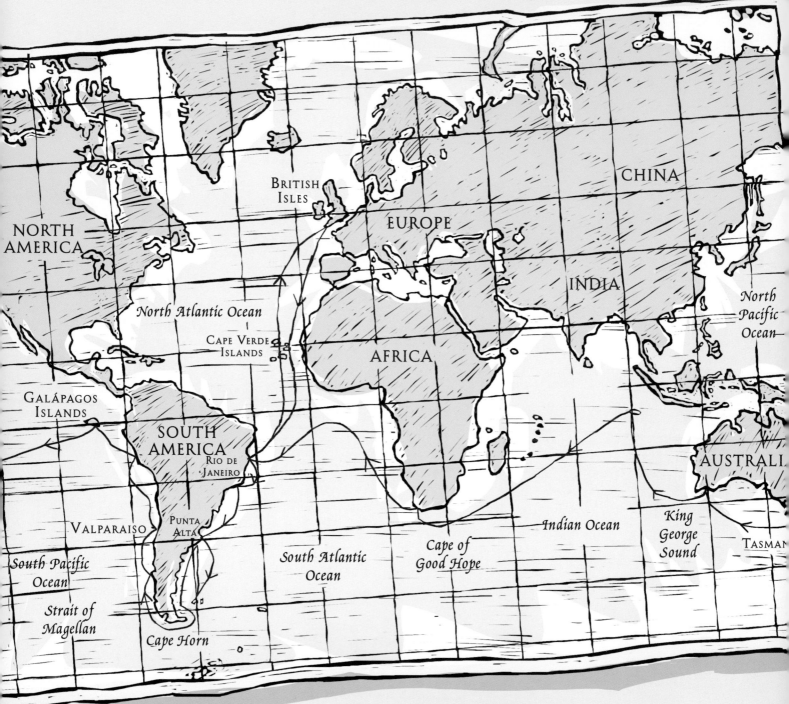

BRITISH
ISLES

CHINA

EUROPE

NORTH
AMERICA

INDIA

North Atlantic Ocean

North
Pacific
Ocean

CAPE VERDE
ISLANDS

AFRICA

GALÁPAGOS
ISLANDS

SOUTH
AMERICA
RIO DE
JANEIRO

AUSTRALI

VALPARAISO

PUNTA
ALTA

Indian Ocean

King
George
Sound

TASMAN

South Pacific
Ocean

South Atlantic
Ocean

Cape of
Good Hope

Strait of
Magellan

Cape Horn

GLOSSARY

epidemic (eh-peh-DEH-mik) a disease that has spread through a large part of one or more countries' populations

evolution (EH-vuh-loo-shun) the slow changing of species over time in order to adapt to environmental conditions

extinct (IK-stingkt) no longer in existence

fossils (FAH-selz) preserved remains or traces of animals or plants that were alive in the past

gauchos (GOW-chohz) cowboys in Argentina

migration (MII-graa-shun) movement from one place to another

natural selection (NA-cheh-rehl seh-LEK-shun) the process by which environmental conditions favor the success of animals or plants with certain traits

naturalist (NA-cheh-rehl-ist) someone who studies animals and plants

niche (nich) a place in an environment supplying what an animal or plant needs to live

pampas (pampuz) grassland area of Argentina

species (SPEE-seez) an animal group that is different from any other animal group

taxidermy (TAK-suh-dur-mee) the art of preserving animals so they look lifelike and will not rot

theory (thir-EE) an explanation that is based on observations and tests

transmutation (trans-myu-TAA-shun) the change from one form into another and the term Darwin used to describe the process of evolution

FOR MORE INFORMATION

To learn more about Charles Darwin and the animals and places that helped him develop his ideas about evolution, check out these books and Web sites.

BOOKS:

Darwin and Evolution for Kids: His Life and Ideas with 21 Activities, by Kristan Lawson (Chicago Review Press, 2003). Investigate further into the life and work of Charles Darwin and conduct hands-on activities related to Darwin's experiences.

Galápagos: Islands of Change, by Lynne Born Myers and Christopher A. Myers (Hyperion, 1995). Explore the islands whose unique animal life helped Darwin develop his theory of evolution. Beautiful photographs and lively text reveal the unusual animal life and the interesting geology of the Galápagos.

WEB SITES:

About Charles Darwin
aboutdarwin.com/index.html
This site is packed with information, photos, and maps that will help you dig deeper into Darwin's life and research.

Destination: Galápagos Islands
pbs.org/safarchive/galapagos.html
Scientific American Frontiers takes you along on a cybertrip to the islands that were an important part of Charles Darwin's research. Don't miss the "For Students" section, packed with experiments and activities.

INDEX